Mr. Aeneas, the fashionable mask-maker.

THE HAPPY HYPOCRITE

The
Happy Hypocrite

by Max Beerbohm

illustrated by George De Hoff

A Star & Elephant Book

The Green Tiger Press

La Jolla • London

1985

This is a new illustrated edition of *The Happy
Hypocrite*, which was originally published in 1896.
The glossary of foreign words and phrases and
archaisms was prepared specially for this edition.
The text appears here in its entirety. Minor editorial
changes have been made to make the text consistent
with American style.

The Green Tiger Press, La Jolla, California 92038
First Edition • First Printing
ISBN: 0-88138-038-5
Library of Congress Catalog Card Number 83-82780

ONE, it is said, of all who reveled with the Regent, was half so wicked as Lord George Hell. I will not trouble my little readers with a long recital of his great naughtiness. But it were well they should know that he was greedy, destructive, and disobedient. I am afraid there is no doubt that he often sat up at Carlton House until long after bedtime, playing at games, and that he generally ate and drank more than was good for him. His fondness for fine clothes was such that he used to dress on weekdays quite as gorgeously as good people dress on Sundays. He was thirty-five years old and a great grief to his parents.

And the worst of it was that he set such a bad example to others. Never, never did he try to conceal his wrongdoing; so that, in time, everyone knew how horrid he was. In fact, I think he was proud of being horrid. Captain Tarleton, in his account of *Contemporary Bucks*, suggested that his Lordship's great Candor was a virtue and should incline us to forgive some of his abominable faults. But, painful as it is to me to dissent from any opinion expressed by one who is now dead, I hold that Candor is good only when it reveals good actions or good sentiments, and that, when it reveals evil, itself is evil, even also.

Lord George Hell did, at last, atone for all his faults, in a way that was never revealed to the world during his lifetime. The reason for his strange and sudden disappearance from that social sphere, in which he had so long moved and never moved again, I will unfold. My little readers will then, I think, acknowledge that any angry judgment they may have passed upon him must be reconsidered and, it may be, withdrawn. I will leave his lordship in their hands. But my plea for him will not be based upon that Candor of his, which some of his friends so much admired. There were, yes! some so weak and so wayward as to think it a fine thing to have an historic title and no scruples. "Here comes George Hell," they would say. "How wicked my lord is looking!" Noblesse oblige, you see, and so an aristocrat should be very careful of his good name. Anonymous naughtiness does little harm.

It is pleasant to record that many persons were inobnoxious to the magic of his title and disapproved of him so strongly that, whenever he entered a room where they happened to be, they would make straight for the door and watch him very severely through the keyhole. Every morning when he strolled up Piccadilly they crossed over to the other side in a compact body, leaving him to the companionship of his bad companions on that which is still called the "shady" side. Lord George— σχετλιος —was quite indifferent to this demonstration. Indeed, he seemed wholly hardened, and when ladies gathered up their skirts as they passed him, he would lightly appraise their ankles.

I am glad I never saw his lordship. They say he was rather like Caligula, with a dash of Sir John Falstaff, and that sometimes on wintry mornings in St. James's Street young children would hush their prattle and cling in disconsolate terror to their nurses' skirts as they saw him come (that vast and fearful gentleman!) with the east wind ruffling the rotund surface of his beaver, ruffling the fur about his neck and wrists, and striking the purple complexion of his cheeks to a still deeper purple. "King Bogey" they called him in the nurseries. In the hours when they too were naughty, their nurses would predict his advent down the chimney or from the linen-press, and then they always "behaved." So that, you see, even the unrighteous are a power for good, in the hands of nurses.

3

"King Bogey" they called him in the nurseries.

It is true that his lordship was a non-smoker—a negative virtue, certainly, and due, even that, I fear, to the fashion of the day—but there the list of his good qualities comes to an abrupt conclusion. He loved with an insatiable love the town and the pleasures of the town, whilst the ennobling influences of our English lakes were quite unknown to him. He used to boast that he had not seen a buttercup for twenty years, and once he called the country "a Fool's Paradise." London was the only place marked on the map of his mind. London gave him all he wished for. Is it not extraordinary to think that he had never spent a happy day nor a day of any kind in Follard Chase, that desirable mansion in Herts, which he had won from Sir Follard Follard, by a chuck of the dice, at Boodle's, on his seventeenth birthday? Always cynical and unkind, he had refused to give the broken baronet his "revenge." Always unkind and insolent, he had offered to install him in the lodge—an offer which was, after a little hesitation, accepted. "On my soul, the man's place is a sinecure," Lord George would say; "he never has to open the gate for me."[1] So rust had covered the great iron gates of Follard Chase, and moss had covered its paths. The deer browsed upon its terraces. There were only wild flowers anywhere. Deep down among the weeds and water lilies of the little stone-rimmed pond he had looked down upon, lay the marble faun, as he had fallen.

Of all the sins of his lordship's life surely not one was more wanton than his neglect of Follard Chase. Some whispered (nor did he ever trouble to deny) that he had won it by foul means, by loaded dice. Indeed no cardplayer in St. James's cheated more persistently than he. As he was rich and had no wife and family to support, and as his luck was always capital, I can offer no excuse for his conduct. At Carlton House, in the presence of many bishops and cabinet ministers, he once dunned the Regent most arrogantly for 5000 guineas out of which he had cheated

[1] Lord Coleraine's Correspondence, page 101.

The Happy Hypocrite 4

 On special occasions, his lordship indulged in odd costumes.

him some months before, and went so far as to declare that he would not leave the house till he got it; whereupon His Royal Highness, with that unfailing tact for which he was ever famous, invited him to stay there as a guest, which, in fact, Lord George did, for several months. After this, we can hardly be surprised when we read that he "seldom sat down to the fashionable game of Limbo with less than four, and sometimes with *as many as seven* aces up his sleeve."[1] We can only wonder that he was tolerated at all.

At Garble's, that nightly resort of titled rips and roisterers, he usually spent the early part of his evenings. Round the illuminated garden, with La Gambogi, the dancer, on his arm and a Bacchic retinue at his heels, he would amble leisurely, clad in Georgian costume, which was not then, of course, fancy dress, as it is now.[2] Now and again, in the midst of his noisy talk, he would crack a joke of the period, or break into a sentimental ballad, dance a little or pick a quarrel. When he tired of such fooling, he would proceed to his box in the tiny alfresco theater and patronize the jugglers, pugilists, playactors and whatever eccentric persons happened to be performing there.

The stars were splendid and the moon as beautiful as a great camellia one night in May, as his lordship laid his arms upon the cushioned ledge of his box and watched the antics of the Merry Dwarf, a little curly-headed creature, whose debut it was. Certainly Garble had found a novelty. Lord George led the applause, and the Dwarf finished his frisking with a pretty song about lovers. Nor was this all. Feats of archery were to follow. In a moment the Dwarf reappeared with a small, gilded bow in

---

[1] *Contemporary Bucks,* vol. 1, page 73.

[2] It would seem, however, that, on special occasions, his lordship indulged in odd costumes. "I have seen him," says Captain Tarleton (vol. 1, p. 69), "attired as a French clown, as a sailor, or in the crimson hose of a Sicilian grandee—*peu beau spectacle.* He never disguised his face, whatever his costume, however."

his hand and a quiverful of arrows slung at his shoulder. Hither and thither he shot these vibrant arrows, very precisely, several into the bark of the acacias that grew about the overt stage, several into the fluted columns of the boxes, two or three to the stars. The audience was delighted. *"Bravo! Bravo Sagittaro!"* murmured Lord George, in the language of La Gambogi, who was at his side. Finally, the waxen figure of a man was carried on by an assistant and propped against the trunk of a tree. A scarf was tied across the eyes of the Merry Dwarf, who stood in a remote corner of the stage. *Bravo* indeed! For the shaft had pierced the waxen figure through the heart, or just where the heart would have been, if the figure had been human and not waxen.

Lord George called for port and champagne and beckoned the bowing homuncle to his box, that he might compliment him on his skill and pledge him in a bumper of the grape.

"On my soul, you have a genius for the bow," his lordship cried with florid condescension. "Come and sit by me, but first let me present you to my divine companion the Signora Gambogi—Virgo and Sagittarius, egad! You may have met on the Zodiac."

"Indeed, I met the Signora many years ago," the Dwarf replied, with a low bow. "But not on the Zodiac, and the Signora perhaps forgets me."

At this speech the Signora flushed angrily, for she was indeed no longer young, and the Dwarf had a childish face. She thought he mocked her; her eyes flashed. Lord George's twinkled rather maliciously.

"Great is the experience of youth," he laughed. "Pray, are you stricken with more than twenty summers?" "With more than I can count," said the Dwarf. "To the health of your lordship!" and he drained his long glass of wine. Lord George replenished it, and asked by what means or miracle he had acquired his mastery of the bow.

Max Beerbohm

He seemed to see a winged and laughing child, in whose hand was a bow.

"By long practice," the little thing rejoined; "long practice on human creatures." And he nodded his curls mysteriously.

"On my heart, you are a dangerous boxmate."

"Your lordship were certainly a good target."

Little liking this joke at his bulk, which really rivaled the Regent's, Lord George turned brusquely in his chair and fixed his eyes upon the stage. This time it was the Gambogi who laughed.

A new operette, *The Fair Captive of Samarcand*, was being enacted, and the frequenters of Garble's were all curious to behold the new debutante, Jenny Mere, who was said to be both pretty and talented. These predictions were surely fulfilled, when the captive peeped from the window of her wooden turret. She looked so pale under her blue turban. Her eyes were dark with fear; her parted lips did not seem capable of speech. "Is it that she is frightened of us?" the audience wondered. "Or of the flashing scimitar of Aphoschaz, the cruel father who holds her captive?" So they gave her loud applause, and when at length she jumped down, to be caught in the arms of her gallant lover, Nissarah, and, throwing aside her Eastern draperies, did a simple dance, in the convention of Columbine, their delight was quite unbounded. She was very young and did not dance very well, it is true, but they forgave her that. And when she turned in the dance and saw her father with his scimitar, their hearts beat swiftly for her. Nor were all eyes tearless when she pleaded with him for her life.

Strangely absorbed, quite callous of his two companions, Lord George gazed over the footlights. He seemed as one who was in a trance. Of a sudden, something shot sharp into his heart. In pain he sprang to his feet and, as he turned, he seemed to see a winged and laughing child, in whose hand was a bow, fly swiftly away into the darkness. At his side was the Dwarf's chair. It was empty. Only La Gambogi was with him, and her dark face was like the face of a fury.

Presently he sank back into his chair, holding one hand to his heart, that still throbbed from the strange transfixion. He breathed very painfully and seemed scarcely conscious of his surroundings. But La Gambogi knew he would pay no more homage to her now, for that the love of Jenny Mere had come into his heart.

When the operette was over, his lovesick lordship snatched up his cloak and went away without one word to the lady at his side. Rudely he brushed aside Count Karoloff and Mr. FitzClarence, with whom he had arranged to play hazard. Of his comrades, his cynicism, his reckless scorn—of all the material of his existence—he was oblivious now. He had no time for penitence or diffident delay. He only knew that he must kneel at the feet of Jenny Mere and ask her to be his wife.

"Miss Mere," said Garble, "is in her room, resuming her ordinary attire. If your lordship deign to await the conclusion of her humble toilet, it shall be my privilege to present her to your lordship. Even now, indeed, I hear her footfall on the stair."

Lord George uncovered his head and with one hand nervously smoothed his rebellious wig.

"Miss Mere, come hither," said Garble. "This is my Lord George Hell that you have pleased, whom by your poor efforts this night will ever be the prime gratification of your passage through the roseate realms of art."

Little Miss Mere who had never seen a lord, except in fancy or in dreams, curtsied shyly and hung her head. With a loud crash Lord George fell on his knees. The manager was greatly surprised, the girl greatly embarrassed. Yet neither of them laughed, for sincerity dignified his posture and sent eloquence from its lips.

"Miss Mere," he cried, "give ear, I pray you, to my poor words, nor spurn me in misprision from the pedestal of your beauty, genius, and virtue. All too conscious, alas! of my presumption in the same, I yet abase myself before you as a suitor for your adorable hand. I grope under the shadow of your raven lashes. I am dazzled in the light of those translucent orbs, your eyes. In the intolerable whirlwind of your fame I faint and am afraid."

"Sir——" the girl began, simply.

"Say 'My Lord,' " said Garble, solemnly.

"My lord, I thank you for your words. They are beautiful. But indeed, indeed, I can never be your bride."

Lord George hid his face in his hands.

"Child," said Mr. Garble, "let not the sun rise e'er you have retracted those wicked words."

"My wealth, my rank, my irremeable love for you, I throw them at your feet," Lord George cried, piteously, "I would wait an hour, a week, a lustrum, even a decade, did you but bid me hope!"

"I can never be your wife," she said, slowly. I can never be the wife of any man whose face is not saintly. Your face, my lord, mirrors, it may be, true love for me, but it is even as a mirror long tarnished by the reflection of this world's vanity. It is even as a tarnished mirror. Do not kneel to me, for I am poor and humble. I was not made for such impetuous wooing. Kneel, if you please, to some greater, gayer lady. As for my love, it is my own, nor can it ever be torn from me, but given, as true love needs be given, freely. Ah, rise from your knees. That man, whose face is wonderful as the faces of the saints, to him I will give my true love."

Miss Mere, though visibly affected, had spoken this speech with a gesture and elocution so superb, that Mr. Garble could not help applauding, deeply though he regretted her attitude towards his honored patron. As for Lord George, he was immobile, a stricken oak. With a sweet look of pity, Miss Mere went her way, and Mr. Garble, with some solicitude, helped his lordship to rise from his knees.

Out into the night, without a word, his lordship went. Above him the stars were still splendid. They seemed to mock the festoons of little lamps, dim now and guttering in the garden of Garble's. What should he do? No thoughts came; only his heart burnt hotly. He stood on the brim of Garble's lake, shallow and artificial as his past life had been. Two swans slept on its surface. The moon shone strangely upon their white, twisted necks. Should he drown himself? There was no one in the garden to prevent him, and in the morning they would find him floating there, one of the noblest of love's victims. The garden would be closed in the evening. There would be no performance in the little theater. It might be that Jenny Mere would mourn him. "Life is a prison, without bars," he murmured, as he walked away.

All night long he strode, knowing not whither, through the mysterious streets and squares of London. The watchmen, to whom his figure was most familiar, gripped their staves at his approach, for they had old reason to fear his wild and riotous habits. He did not heed them. Through that dim conflict between darkness and day, which is ever waged silently over our sleep, Lord George strode on in the deep absorption of his love and of his despair. At dawn he found himself on the outskirts of a little wood in Kensington. A rabbit rushed past him through the dew. Birds were fluttering in the branches. The leaves were tremulous with the presage of day, and the air was full of the sweet scent of hyacinths.

How cool the country was! It seemed to cure the feverish maladies of his soul and consecrate his love. In the fair light of the dawn he began to shape the means of winning Jenny Mere, that he had conceived in the desperate hours of the night. Soon an old woodman passed by, and, with rough courtesy, showed him the path that would lead him quickest to the town. He was loath to leave the wood. With Jenny, he thought, he would live always in the country. And he picked a posy of wildflowers for her.

His *rentrée* into the still silent town strengthened his Arcadian resolves. He, who had seen the town so often in its hours of sleep, had never noticed how sinister its whole aspect was. In

Max Beerbohm

its narrow streets the white houses rose on either side of him like cliffs of chalk. He hurried swiftly along the unswept pavement. How had he loved this city of evil secrets?

At last he came to St. James's Square, to the hateful door of his own house. Shadows lay like memories in every corner of the dim hall. Through the window of his room a sunbeam slanted across his smooth, white bed, and fell ghastly on the ashen grate.

Life is a prison without bars.

It was a bright morning in Old Bond Street, and fat little Mr. Aeneas, the fashionable mask-maker, was sunning himself at the door of his shop. His window was lined as usual with all kinds of masks—beautiful masks with pink cheeks, and absurd masks with protuberant chins; curious πρόσωπα copied from old tragic models; masks of paper for children, of fine silk for ladies, and of leather for working men; bearded or beardless, gilded or waxen (most of them, indeed, were waxen), big or little masks. And in the middle of this vain galaxy hung the presentment of a Cyclops's face, carved cunningly of gold, with a great sapphire in its brow.

The sun gleamed brightly on the window and on the bald head and varnished shoes of fat little Mr. Aeneas. It was too early for any customers to come and Mr. Aeneas seemed to be greatly enjoying his leisure in the fresh air. He smiled complacently as he stood there, and well he might, for he was a great artist, and was patronized by several crowned heads and not a few of the nobility. Only the evening before, Mr. Brummell had come into his shop and ordered a light summer mask, wishing to evade for a time the jealous vigilance of Lady Otterton. It pleased Mr. Aeneas to think that his art made him the recipient of so many high secrets. He smiled as he thought of the titled spendthrifts, who, at this moment, *perdus* behind his masterpieces, passed unscathed among their creditors. He was the secular confessor of his day, always able to give absolution. An unique position!

The street was as quiet as a village street. At an open window over the way, a handsome lady, wrapped in a muslin peignoir, sat sipping her cup of chocolate. It was La Signora Gambogi, and Mr. Aeneas made her many elaborate bows. This morning, how-ever, her thoughts seemed far away, and she did not notice the little man's polite efforts. Nettled at her negligence, Mr. Aeneas was on the point of retiring into his shop, when he saw Lord George Hell hastening up the street, with a posy of wildflowers in his hand.

La Signora Gambogi

"His lordship is up betimes!" he said to himself. "An early visit to la Signora, I suppose."

Not so, however. His lordship came straight towards the mask-shop. Once he glanced up at the Signora's window and looked deeply annoyed when he saw her sitting there. He came quickly into the shop.

"I want the mask of a saint," he said.

"Mask of a saint, my lord? Certainly!" said Mr. Aeneas, briskly. "With or without halo? His Grace the Bishop of St. Aldreds always wears his with a halo. Your lordship does not wish for a halo? Certainly! If your lordship will allow me to take the measurement——"

"I must have the mask today," Lord George said. "Have you none ready-made?"

"Ah, I see. Required for immediate wear," murmured Mr. Aeneas, dubiously. "You see, your lordship takes a rather large size." And he looked at the floor.

"Julius!" he cried suddenly to his assistant, who was putting finishing touches to a mask of Barbarossa which the young king of Zürremburg was to wear at his coronation the following week. "Julius! Do you remember the saint's mask we made for Mr. Ripsby, a couple of years ago?"

"Yes, sir," said the boy. "It's stored upstairs."

"I thought so," replied Mr. Aeneas. "Mr. Ripsby only had it on hire. Step upstairs, Julius, and bring it down. I fancy it is just what your lordship would wish. Spiritual, yet handsome."

"Is it a mask that is even as a mirror of true love?" Lord George asked gravely.

"It was made precisely as such," the mask-maker answered. "In fact it was made for Mr. Ripsby to wear at his silver wedding, and was very highly praised by the relatives of Mrs. Ripsby. Will your lordship step into my little room?"

So Mr. Aeneas led the way to his parlor behind the shop. He was elated by the distinguished acquisition to his clientele, for hitherto Lord George had never patronized his business. He bustled round his parlor and insisted that his lordship should take a chair and a pinch from his snuffbox, while the saint's mask was being found.

Lord George's eye traveled along the rows of framed letters from great personages, which lined the walls. He did not see them though, for he was calculating the chances that La Gambogi had not observed him, as he entered the mask-shop. He had come down so early that he thought she would be still abed. That sinister old proverb, *La jalouse se lève de bonne heure*, rose in his memory. His eye fell unconsciously on a large, round mask made of dull silver, with the features of a human face traced over its surface in faint filigree.

"Your lordship wonders what mask that is!" chirped Mr. Aeneas, tapping the thing with one of his little fingernails.

"What is that mask?" Lord George murmured, absently.

"I ought not to divulge, my lord," said the mask-maker. "But I know your lordship would respect a professional secret, a secret of which I am pardonably proud. This," he said, "is a mask for the sun-god, Apollo, whom heaven bless!"

"You astound me," said Lord George.

"Of no less a person, I do assure you. When Jupiter, his father, made him lord of the day, Apollo craved that he might sometimes see the doings of mankind in the hours of nighttime. Jupiter granted so reasonable a request, and when next Apollo had passed over the sky and hidden in the sea, and darkness had fallen on all the world, he raised his head above the waters that he might watch the doings of mankind in the hours of nighttime. But," Mr. Aeneas added, with a smile, "his bright countenance made light all the darkness. Men rose from their couches or from their revels, wondering that day was so soon come, and went to their work. And Apollo sank weeping into the sea. 'Surely,' he cried, 'it is a bitter thing that I alone, of all the gods, may not watch the world in the hours of nighttime. For in those hours,

as I am told, men are even as gods are. They spill the wine and are wreathed with roses. Their daughters dance in the light of torches. They laugh to the sound of flutes. On their long couches they lie down at last and sleep comes to kiss their eyelids. None of these things may I see. Wherefore the brightness of my beauty is even as a curse to me and I would put it from me.' And as he wept, Vulcan said to him, 'I am not the least cunning of the gods, nor the least pitiful. Do not weep, for I will give you that which shall end your sorrow. Nor need you put from you the brightness of your beauty.' And Vulcan made a mask of dull silver and fastened it across his brother's face. And that night, thus masked, the sun-god rose from the sea and watched the doings of mankind in the nighttime. Nor any longer were men abashed by his bright beauty, for it was hidden by the mask of silver. Those whom he had so often seen haggard over their daily tasks, he saw feasting now and wreathed with red roses. He heard them laugh to the sound of flutes, as their daughters danced in the red light of torches. And when at length they lay down upon their soft couches and sleep kissed their eyelids, he sank back into the sea and hid his mask under a little rock in the bed of the sea. Nor have men ever known that Apollo watches them often in the nighttime, but fancied it to be some pale goddess.

"I myself have always thought it was Diana," said Lord George Hell.

"An error, my lord!" said Mr. Aeneas, with a smile. *"Ecce signum!"* And he tapped the mask of dull silver.

"Strange!" said his lordship. "And pray how comes it that Apollo has ordered of *you* this new mask?"

"He has always worn twelve new masks every year, inasmuch as no mask can endure for many nights the near brightness of his face, before which even a mask of the best and purest silver soon tarnishes, and wears away. Centuries ago, Vulcan tired of making so very many masks. And so Apollo sent Mercury down

The Happy Hypocrite 20

to Athens, to the shop of Phoron, a Phoenician mask-maker of great skill. Phoron made Apollo's masks for many years, and every month Mercury came to his shop for a new one. When Phoron died, another artist was chosen, and, when he died, another, and so on through all the ages of the world. Conceive, my lord, my pride and pleasure when Mercury flew into my shop, one night last year, and made me Apollo's warrant-holder. It is the highest privilege that any mask-maker can desire. And when I die," said Mr. Aeneas, with some emotion, "Mercury will confer my post upon another."

"And do they pay you for your labor?" Lord George asked.

Mr. Aeneas drew himself up to his full height, such as it was. "In Olympus, my lord," he said, "they have no currency. For any mask-maker, so high a privilege is its own reward. Yet the sun-god is generous. He shines more brightly into my shop than into any other. Nor does he suffer his rays to melt any waxen mask made by me, until its wearer doff it and it be done with." At this moment Julius came in with the Ripsby mask. "I must ask your lordship's pardon, for having kept you so long," pleaded Mr. Aeneas. "But I have a large store of old masks and they are imperfectly catalogued."

It certainly was a beautiful mask, with its smooth, pink cheeks and devotional brows. It was made of the finest wax. Lord George took it gingerly in his hands and tried it on his face. It fitted *à merveille.*

"Is the expression exactly as your lordship would wish?" asked Mr. Aeneas.

Lord George laid it on the table and studied it intently. "I wish it were more as a perfect mirror of true love," he said at length. "It is too calm, too contemplative."

"Easily remedied!" said Mr. Aeneas. Selecting a fine pencil, he deftly drew they eyebrows closer to each other. With a brush steeped in some scarlet pigment, he put a fuller curve upon the lips. And, behold! it was the mask of a saint who loves dearly. Lord George's heart throbbed with pleasure.

"And for how long does your lordship wish to wear it?" asked Mr. Aeneas.

"I must wear it until I die," replied Lord George.

"Kindly be seated then, I pray," rejoined the little man. "For I must apply the mask with great care. Julius, you will assist me!"

So, while Julius heated the inner side of the waxen mask over a little lamp, Mr. Aeneas stood over Lord George gently smearing his features with some sweet-scented pomade. Then he took the mask and powdered its inner side, quite soft and warm now, with a fluffy puff. "Keep quite still, for one instant," he said, and clapped the mask firmly on his lordship's upturned face. So soon as he was sure of its perfect adhesion, he took from his assistant's hand a silver file and a little wooden spatula, with which he proceeded to pare down the edge of the mask, where it joined the neck and ears. At length, all traces of the "join" were obliterated. It remained only to arrange the curls of the lordly wig over the waxen brow.

The disguise was done. When Lord George looked through the eyelets of his mask into the mirror that was placed in his hand, he saw a face that was saintly, itself a mirror of true love. How wonderful it was! He felt his past was a dream. He felt he was a new man indeed. His voice went strangely through the mask's parted lips, as he thanked Mr. Aeneas.

"Proud to have served your lordshp," said that little worthy, pocketing his fee of fifty guineas, while he bowed his customer out.

When he reached the street, Lord George nearly uttered a curse through those sainted lips of his. For there, right in his way, stood La Gambogi, with a small, pink parasol. She laid her hand upon his sleeve and called him softly by his name. He passed her by without a word. Again she confronted him.

"I cannot let go so handsome a lover," she laughed, "even though he spurn me! Do not spurn me, George. Give me your posy of wildflowers. Why, you never looked so lovingly at me in all your life!"

"Madam," said Lord George, sternly, "I have not the honor to know you." And he passed on.

The lady gazed after her lost lover with the blackest hatred in her eyes. Presently she beckoned across the road to a certain spy.

And the spy followed him.

Lord George, greatly agitated, had turned into Piccadilly. It was horrible to have met this garish embodiment of his past on the very threshold of his fair future. The mask-maker's elevating talk about the gods, followed by the initiative ceremony of his saintly mask, had driven all discordant memories from his love-thoughts of Jenny Mere. And then to be met by La Gambogi! It might be that, after his stern words, she would not seek to cross his path again. Surely she would not seek to mar his sacred love. Yet, he knew her dark, Italian nature, her passion of revenge. What was the line in Virgil? *Spretasque*—something. Who knew but that somehow, sooner or later, she might come between him and his love?

He was about to pass Lord Barrymore's mansion. Count Karoloff and Mr. FitzClarence were lounging in one of the lower windows. Would they know him under his mask? Thank God! they did not. They merely laughed as he went by, and Mr. FitzClarence cried in a mocking voice, "Sing us a hymn, Mr. Whatever-your-saint's-name-is!" The mask, then, at least, was perfect. Jenny Mere would not know him. He need fear no one but La Gambogi. But would not she betray his secret? He sighed.

That night he was going to visit Garble's and to declare his love to the little actress. He never doubted that she would love him for his saintly face. Had she not said, "That man whose face

23 *Max Beerbohm*

is wonderful as are the faces of the saints, to him I will give my true love"? She could not say now that his face was as a tarnished mirror of love. She would smile on him. She would be his bride. But would La Gambogi be at Garble's?

The operette would not be over before ten that night. The clock in Hyde Park Gate told him it was not yet ten—ten of the morning. Twelve whole hours to wait, before he could fall at Jenny's feet! "I cannot spend that time in this place of memories," he thought. So he hailed a yellow cabriolet and bade the jarvey drive him out to the village of Kensington.

When they came to the little wood where he had been but a few hours ago, Lord George dismissed the jarvey. The sun, that had risen as he stood there thinking of Jenny, shone down on his altered face, but, though it shone very fiercely, it did not melt his waxen features. The old woodman, who had shown him his way, passed by under a load of faggots and did not know him. He wandered among the trees. It was a lovely wood.

Presently he came to the bank of that tiny stream, the Ken, which still flowed there in those days. On the moss of its bank he lay down and let its water ripple over his hand. Some bright pebble glistened under the surface, and, as he peered down at it, he saw in the stream the reflection of his mask. A great shame filled him that he should so cheat the girl he loved. Behind that fair mask there would still be the evil face that had repelled her. Could he be so base as to decoy her into love of that most ingenious deception? He was filled with a great pity for her, with a hatred of himself. And yet, he argued, was the mask indeed a mean trick? Surely it was a secret symbol of his true repentance and of his true love. His face was evil, because his life had been evil. He had seen a gracious girl, and of a sudden his very soul had changed. His face alone was the same as it had been. It was not just that his face should be evil still.

There was the faint sound of someone sighing. Lord George looked up, and there, on the further bank, stood Jenny Mere, watching him. As their eyes met, she blushed and hung her head. She looked like nothing but a tall child, as she stood there, with her straight, limp frock of lilac cotton and her sunburnt straw bonnet. He dared not speak; he could only gaze at her. Suddenly there perched astride the bough of a tree, at her side, that winged and laughing child, in whose hand was a bow. Before Lord George could warn her, an arrow had flashed down and vanished in her heart, and Cupid had flown away.

No cry of pain did she utter, but stretched out her arms to her lover, with a glad smile. He leapt quite lightly over the little stream and knelt at her feet. It seemed more fitting that he should kneel before the gracious thing he was unworthy of. But she, knowing only that his face was as the face of a great saint, bent over him and touched him with her hand.

"Surely," she said, "you are that good man for whom I have waited. Therefore do not kneel to me, but rise and suffer me to kiss your hand. For my love of you is lowly, and my heart is all yours."

But he answered, looking up into her fond eyes, "Nay, you are a queen, and I must needs kneel in your presence."

And she shook her head wistfully, and she knelt down, also, in her tremulous ecstasy, before him. And as they knelt, the one to the other, the tears came into her eyes, and he kissed her. Though the lips that he pressed to her lips were only waxen, he thrilled with happiness, in that mimic kiss. He held her close to him in his arms, and they were silent in the sacredness of their love.

From his breast he took the posy of wildflowers that he had gathered.

"They are for you," he whispered, "I gathered them for you, hours ago, in this wood. See! They are not withered."

But she was perplexed by his words and said to him, blushing, "How was it for me that you gathered them, though you had never seen me?"

25   *Max Beerbohm*

"I gathered them for you," he answered, "knowing I should soon see you. How was it that you, who had never seen me, yet waited for me?"

"I waited, knowing I should see you at last." And she kissed the posy and put it at her breast.

And they rose from their knees and went into the wood, walking hand in hand. As they went, he asked the names of the flowers that grew under their feet. "These are primroses," she would say. "Did you not know? And these are ladies' feet, and these forget-me-nots. And that white flower, climbing up the trunks of the trees and trailing down so prettily from the branches, is called Astyanax. These little yellow things are buttercups. Did you not know?" And she laughed.

"I know the names of none of the flowers," he said.

She looked up into his face and said timidly, "Is it worldly and wrong of me to have loved the flowers? Ought I to have thought more of those higher things that are unseen?"

His heart smote him. He could not answer her simplicity.

"Surely the flowers are good, and did not you gather this posy for me?" she pleaded. "But if you do not love them, I must not. And I will try to forget their names. For I must try to be like you in all things."

"Love the flowers always," he said. "And teach me to love them."

So she told him all about the flowers, how some grew very slowly and others bloomed in a night; how clever the convolvulus was at climbing, and how shy violets were, and why honeycups had folded petals. She told him of the birds, too, that sang in the wood, how she knew them all by their voices. "That is a chaffinch singing. Listen!" she said. And she tried to imitate its note, that her lover might remember. All the birds, according to her, were good, except the cuckoo, and whenever she heard him sing she would stop her ears, lest she should forgive him for robbing the nests. "Every day," she said, "I have come to the wood, because I was lonely, and it seemed to pity me. But now I have you. And it is glad."

She clung closer to his arm, and he kissed her. She pushed back her straw bonnet, so that it dangled from her neck by its ribands, and laid her little head against his shoulder. For a while he forgot his treachery to her, thinking only of his love and her love. Suddenly she said to him, "Will you try not to be angry with me, if I tell you something? It is something that will seem dreadful to you."

"Pauvrette," he answered, "you cannot have anything very dreadful to tell."

"I am very poor," she said, "and every night I dance in a theater. It is the only thing I can do to earn my bread. Do you despise me because I dance?" She looked up shyly at him and saw that his face was full of love for her and not angry.

"Do you like dancing?" he asked.

"I hate it," she answered, quickly. "I hate it indeed. Yet—— tonight, alas! I must dance again in the theater."

"You need never dance again," said her lover. "I am rich and I will pay them to release you. You shall dance only for me. Sweetheart, it cannot be much more than noon. Let us go into the town, while there is time, and you shall be made my bride, and I your bridegroom, this very day. Why should you and I be lonely?"

"I do not know," she said.

So they walked back through the wood, taking a narrow path which Jenny said would lead them quickest to the village. And, as they went, they came to a tiny cottage, with a garden that was full of flowers. The old woodman was leaning over its paling, and he nodded to them as they passed.

"I often used to envy the woodman," said Jenny, "living in that dear little cottage."

27 *Max Beerbohm*

"Let us live there, then," said Lord George. And he went back and asked the old man if he were not unhappy, living there alone.

" 'Tis a poor life here for me," the old man answered. "No folk come to the wood, except little children, now and again, to play, or lovers like you. But they seldom notice me. And in winter I am alone with Jack Frost. Old men love merrier company than that. Oh! I shall die in the snow with my faggots on my back. A poor life here!"

"I will give you gold for your cottage and whatever is in it, and then you can go and live happily in town," Lord George said. And he took from his coat a note for two hundred guineas, and held it across the palings.

"Lovers are poor, foolish derry-docks," the old man muttered. "But I thank you kindly, sir. This little sum will keep me cozy, as long as I last. Come into the cottage as soon as can be. It's a lonely place and does my heart good to depart from it."

"We are going to be married this afternoon, in the town," said Lord George. "We will come straight back to our home."

"May you be happy!" replied the woodman. "You'll find me gone when you come."

And the lovers thanked him and went their way.

"Are you very rich?" Jenny asked. "Ought you to have bought the cottage for that great price?"

"Would you love me as much if I were quite poor, little Jenny?" he asked her after a pause.

"I did not know you were rich when I saw you across the stream," she said.

And in his heart Lord George made a good resolve. He would put away from him all his worldly possessions. All the money that he had won at the clubs, fairly or foully, all that hideous accretion of gold guineas, he would distribute among the comrades he had impoverished. As he walked, with the sweet and trustful girl at his side, the vague record of his infamy assailed

The Happy Hypocrite 28

him, and a look of pain shot behind his smooth mask. He would atone. He would shun no sacrifice that might cleanse his soul. All his fortune he would put from him. Follard Chase he would give back to Sir Follard. He would sell his house in St. James's Square. He would keep some little part of his patrimony, enough for him in the wood, with Jenny, but no more.

"I shall be quite poor, Jenny," he said.

And they talked of the things that lovers love to talk of, how happy they would be together and how economical. As they were passing Herbert's pastry shop, which as my little readers know, still stands in Kensington, Jenny looked up rather wistfully into her lover's ascetic face.

"Should you think me greedy," she asked him, "if I wanted a bun? They have beautiful buns here!"

Buns! The simple word started latent memories of his childhood. Jenny was only a child, after all. Buns! He had forgotten what they were like. And as they looked at the piles of variegated cakes in the window, he said to her, "Which are buns, Jenny? I should like to have one, too."

"I almost afraid of you," she said. "You must despise me so. Are you so good that you deny yourself all the vanity and pleasure that most people love? It is wonderful not to know what buns are! The round, brown, shiny cakes, with little raisins in them, are buns."

So he bought two beautiful buns, and they sat together in the shop, eating them. Jenny bit hers rather diffidently, but was reassured when he said that they must have buns very often in the cottage. Yes! he, the famous toper and gourmet of St. James's, relished this homely fare, as it passed through the insensible lips of his mask to his palate. He seemed to rise, from the consumption of his bun, a better man.

But there was no time to lose now. It was already past two o'clock. So he got a chaise from the inn opposite the pastry shop,

Max Beerbohm

and they were swiftly driven to Doctors' Commons. There he purchased a special license. When the clerk asked him to write his name upon it, he hesitated. What name should he assume? Under a mask he had wooed this girl, under an unreal name he must make her his bride. He loathed himself for a trickster. He had vilely stolen from her the love she would not give him. Even now, should he not confess himself the man whose face had frightened her, and go his way? And yet, surely, it was not just that he, whose soul was transfigured, should bear his old name. Surely George Hell was dead, and his name had died with him. So he dipped a pen in the ink and wrote "George Heaven," for want of a better name. And Jenny wrote "Jenny Mere" beneath it.

An hour later they were married according to the simple rites of a dear little registry office in Covent Garden.

And in the cool evening they went home.

An hour later, they were married according to the simple rites
of a dear little registry office in Covent Garden.
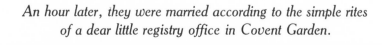

In the cottage that had been the woodman's they had a wonderful honeymoon. No king and queen in any palace of gold were happier than they. For them their tiny cottage was a palace, and the flowers that filled the garden were their courtiers. Long and careless and full of kisses were the days of their reign.

Sometimes, indeed, strange dreams troubled Lord George's sleep. Once he dreamt that he stood knocking and knocking at the great door of a castle. It was a bitter night. The frost enveloped him. No one came. Presently he heard a footstep in the hall beyond, and a pair of frightened eyes peered at him through the grill. Jenny was scanning his face. She would not open to him. With tears and wild words he beseeched her, but she would not open to him. Then, very stealthily, he crept round the castle and found a small casement in the wall. It was open. He climbed swiftly, quietly through it. In the darkness of the room someone ran to him and kissed him gladly. It was Jenny. With a cry of joy and shame he awoke. By his side lay Jenny, sleeping like a little child.

After all, what was a dream to him? It could not mar the reality of his daily happiness. He cherished his true penitence for the evil he had done in the past. The past! That was indeed the only unreal thing that lingered in his life. Every day its substance dwindled, grew fainter yet, as he lived his rustic honeymoon. Had he not utterly put it from him? Had he not, a few hours after his marriage, written to his lawyer, declaring solemnly that he, Lord George Hell, had forsworn the world, that he was where no man would find him, that he desired all his worldly goods to be distributed, thus and thus, among these and those of his companions? By this testament he had verily atoned for the wrong he had done, had made himself dead indeed to the world.

No address had he written upon this document. Though its injunctions were final and binding, it could betray no clue of his hiding-place. For the rest, no one would care to seek him out.

The Happy Hypocrite   32

He, who had done no good to human creature, would pass unmourned out of memory. The clubs, doubtless, would laugh and puzzle over his strange recantations, envious of whomever he enriched. They would say 'twas a good riddance of a rogue and soon forget him.[1] But she, whose prime patron he had been, who had loved him in her vile fashion, La Gambogi, would she forget him easily, like the rest? As the sweet days went by, her specter, also, grew fainter and less formidable. She knew his mask indeed, but how should she find him in the cottage near Kensington? *Devia dulcedo latebrarum!* He was safe hidden with his bride. As for the Italian, she might search and search—or had forgotten him, in the arms of another lover.

Yes! Few and faint became the blemishes of his honeymoon. At first, he had felt that his waxen mask, though it had been the means of his happiness, was rather a barrier 'twixt him and his bride. Though it was sweet to kiss her through it, to look at her through it with loving eyes, yet there were times when it incommoded him with its mockery. Could he but put it from him! yet, that, of course, could not be. He must wear it all his life. And so, as days went by he grew reconciled to his mask. No longer did he feel it jarring on his face. It seemed to become an integral part of him, and, for all its rigid material, it did forsooth express the one emotion that filled him, true love. The face, for whose sake Jenny gave him her heart, could not but be dear to this George Heaven, also.

Every day chastened him with its joy. They lived a very simple life, he and Jenny. They rose betimes, like the birds, for whose

---

[1] I would refer my little readers once more to the pages of *Contemporary Bucks,* where Captain Tarleton speculates upon the sudden disappearance of Lord George Hell and describes its effect on the town. "Not even the shrewdest," says he, "even gave a guess that would throw a ray of revealing light on the *disparition* of this profligate man. It was supposed that he carried off with him a little dancer from Garble's, at which *haunt of pleasantry* he was certainly on the night he vanished, and whither the young lady never returned again. Garble declared he had been compensated for her perfidy, but that he was sure she had not succumbed to his lordship, having in fact rejected him soundly. Did his lordship, say the cronies, take his life—and hers? *Il n'y a pas d'épreuve.*

33 *Max Beerbohm*

goodness they both had so sincere a love. Bread and honey and little strawberries were their morning fare, and in the evening they had seed cake and dewberry wine. Jenny herself made the wine and her husband drank it, in strict moderation, never more than two glasses. He thought it tasted far better than the Regent's cherry brandy, or the Tokay at Brooks's. Of these treasured topes he had, indeed, nearly forgotten the taste. The wine made from wild berries by his little bride was august enough for his palate. Sometimes, after they had dined thus, he would play the flute to her upon the moonlit lawn, or tell her of the great daisy-chain he was going to make for her on the morrow, or sit silently by her side, listening to the nightingale, till bedtime. So admirably simple were their days.

One morning, as he was helping Jenny to water the flowers, he said to her suddenly, "Sweetheart, we had forgotten!"

"What was there we should forget?" asked Jenny, looking up from her task.

" 'Tis the mensiversary of our wedding," her husband answered gravely. "We must not let it pass without some celebration."

"No, indeed," she said, "we must not. What shall we do?"

Between them they decided upon an unusual feast. They would go into the village and buy a bag of beautiful buns and eat them in the afternoon. So soon, then, as all the flowers were watered, they set forth to Herbert's shop, bought the buns and returned home in very high spirits, George bearing a paper bag that held

"The *most astonishing* matter is that the runaway should have written out a complete will, restoring all money he had won at cards, etc., etc. This certainly corroborates the opinion that he was seized with a sudden repentance and fled over the seas to a foreign monastery, where he died at last in *religious silence.* That's as it may, but many a spendthrift found his pocket clinking with guineas, a not unpleasant sound, I declare. The Regent himself was benefited by the odd will, and old Sir Follard Follard found himself once more in the ancestral home he had forfeited. As for Lord George's mansion in St. James's Square, that was sold with all its appurtenances, and the money fetched by the sale, no bagatelle, was given to various good objects, according to my lord's stated wishes. Well, many of us blessed his name—we had cursed it often enough. Peace to his ashes, in whatever urn they may be resting, on the billows of whatever ocean they float!"

35   *On the rustic table Jenny built up the buns, one above the other,*
till they looked like a tall pagoda.

no less than twelve of the wholesome delicacies. Under the plane tree on the lawn Jenny sat her down, and George stretched himself at her feet. They were loath to enjoy their feast too soon. They dallied in childish anticipation. On the little rustic table Jenny built up the buns, one above the other, till they looked like a tall pagoda. When, very gingerly, she had crowned the structure with the twelfth bun, her husband looking on with admiration, she clapped her hands and danced about it. She laughed so loudly (for, though she was only sixteen years old, she had a great sense of humor), that the table shook, and alas! the pagoda tottered and fell to the lawn. Swift as a kitten, Jenny chased the buns, as they rolled, hither and thither, over the grass, catching them deftly with her hand. Then she came back, flushed and merry under her tumbled hair, with her arm full of buns. She began to put them back in the paper bag.

"Dear husband," she said, looking down to him, "why do not you smile too at my folly? Your grave face rebukes me. Smile, or I shall think I vex you. Please smile a little."

But the mask could not smile, of course. It was made for a mirror of true love, and it was grave and immobile. "I am very much amused, dear," he said, "at the fall of the buns, but my lips will not curve to a smile. Love of you has bound them in spell."

"But I can laugh, though I love you. I do not understand." And she wondered. He took her hand in his and stroked it gently, wishing it were possible to smile. Some day, perhaps, she would tire of this monotonous gravity, this rigid sweetness. It was not strange that she should long for a little facile expression. They sat silently.

"Jenny, what is it?" he whispered suddenly. For Jenny, with wide-open eyes, was gazing over his head, across the lawn. "Why do you look frightened?"

"There is a strange woman smiling at me across the palings," she said. "I do not know her."

Her husband's heart sank. Somehow, he dared not turn his head to the intruder. He dreaded who she might be.

"She is nodding to me," said Jenny. "I think she is foreign, for she has an evil face."

"Do not notice her," he whispered. "Does she look evil?"

"Very evil and very dark. She has a pink parasol. Her teeth are like ivory."

"Do not notice her. Think! It is the mensiversary of our wedding, dear!"

"I wish she would not smile at me. Her eyes are like bright blots of ink."

"Let us eat our beautiful buns!"

"Oh, she is coming in!" George heard the latch of the gate jar. "Forbid her to come in!" whispered Jenny, "I am afraid!" He heard the jar of heels on the gravel path. Yet he dared not turn. Only he clasped Jenny's hand more tightly, as he waited for the voice. It was La Gambogi's.

"Pray, pray, pardon me! I could not mistake the back of so old a friend."

With the courage of despair, George turned and faced the woman.

"Even," she smiled, "though his face has changed marvelously."

"Madam," he said, rising to his full height and stepping between her and his bride, "begone, I command you, from the garden. I do not see what good is to be served by the renewal of our acquaintance."

"Acquaintance!" murmured La Gambogi, with an arch of her beetle-brows. "Surely we were friends, rather, nor is my esteem for you so dead that I would crave estrangement."

"Madam," rejoined Lord George, with a tremor in his voice, "you see me happy, living very peacefully with my bride—"

"To whom, I beseech you, old friend, present me."

"I would not," he said hotly, "desecrate her sweet name by speaking it with so infamous a name as yours."

37 *Max Beerbohm*

"Your choler hurts me, old friend," said La Gambogi, sinking composedly upon the garden-seat and smoothing the silk of her skirts.

"Jenny," said George, "then do you retire, pending this lady's departure, to the cottage." But Jenny clung to his arm. "I were less frightened at your side," she whispered. "Do not send me away!"

"Suffer her pretty presence," said La Gambogi. "Indeed I am come this long way from the heart of the town, that I may see her, no less than you, George. My wish is only to befriend her. Why should she not set you a mannerly example, giving me welcome? Come and sit by me, little bride, for I have things to tell you. Though you reject my friendship, give me, at least, the slight courtesy of audience. I will not detain you overlong, will be gone very soon. Are you expecting guests, George? *On dirait une masque champêtre!*" She eyed the couple critically. "Your wife's mask," she said, "is even better than yours."

"What does she mean?" whispered Jenny. "Oh, send her away!"

"Serpent," was all George could say, "crawl from our Eden, ere you poison with your venom its fairest denizen."

La Gambogi rose. "Even *my* pride," she cried passionately, "knows certain bounds. I have been forbearing, but even in *my* zeal for friendship I will not be called 'serpent.' I will indeed begone from this rude place. Yet, ere I go, there is a boon I will deign to beg. Show me, oh show me but once again, the dear face I have so often caressed, the lips that were dear to me!"

George started back.

"What does she mean?" whispered Jenny.

"In memory of our old friendship," continued La Gambogi, "grant me this piteous favor. Show me your own face but for one instant, and I vow I will never again remind you that I live. Intercede for me, little bride. Bid him unmask for me. You have more authority over him than I. Doff his mask with your own uxorious fingers."

"What does she mean?" was the refrain of poor Jenny.

"If," said George, gazing sternly at his traitress, "you do not go now, of your own will, I must drive you, man though I am, violently from the garden."

"Doff your mask and I am gone."

George made a step of menace towards her.

"False saint!" she shrieked, "then *I* will unmask you."

Like a panther she sprang upon him and clawed at his waxen cheeks. Jenny fell back, mute with terror. Vainly did George try to free himself from the hideous assailant, who writhed round and round him, clawing, clawing at what Jenny fancied to be his face. With a wild cry, Jenny fell upon the furious creature and tried, with all her childish strength, to release her dear one. The combatives swayed to and fro, a revulsive trinity. There was a loud pop, as though some great cork had been withdrawn, and La Gambogi recoiled. She had torn away the mask. It lay before her upon the lawn, upturned to the sky.

George stood motionless. La Gambogi stared up into his face, and her dark flush died swiftly away. For there, staring back at her, was the man she had unmasked, but, lo! his face was even as his mask had been. Line for line, feature for feature, it was the same. 'Twas a saint's face.

"Madam," he said, in the calm voice of despair, "your cheek may well blanch, when you regard the ruin you have brought upon me. Nevertheless do I pardon you. The gods have avenged, through you, the imposture I wrought upon one who was dear to me. For that unpardonable sin I am punished. As for my poor bride, whose love I stole by the means of that waxen semblance, of her I cannot ask pardon. Ah, Jenny, Jenny, do not look at me. Turn your eyes from the foul reality that I dissembled." He shuddered and hid his face in his hands. "Do not look at me. I will go from the garden. Nor will I ever curse you with the odious spectacle of my face. Forget me, forget me."

39 *Max Beerbohm*

"False saint!" she shrieked. "Then I will unmask you."

But, as he turned to go, Jenny laid her hands upon his wrists and besought him that he would look at her. "For indeed," she said, "I am bewildered by your strange words. Why did you woo me under a mask? And why do you imagine I could love you less dearly, seeing your own face?"

He looked into her eyes. On their violet surface he saw the tiny reflection of his own face. He was filled with joy and wonder.

"Surely," said Jenny, "your face is even dearer to me, even fairer, than the semblance that hid it and deceived me. I am not angry. 'Twas well that you veiled from me the full glory of your face, for indeed I was not worthy to behold it too soon. But I am your wife now. Let me look always at your own face. Let the time of my probation be over. Kiss me with your own lips."

So he look her in his arms, as though she had been a little child, and kissed her with his own lips. She put her arms round his neck, and he was happier than he had ever been. They were alone in the garden now. Nor lay the mask any longer upon the lawn, for the sun had melted it.

GLOSSARY OF FOREIGN WORDS
AND PHRASES
AND ARCHAISMS

à merveille (French) — marvelously

Bravo! Bravo Sagittaro! (Italian) — Hooray! Brave archer!

Devia dulcedo latebrarum (Latin) — the out-of-the-way sweetness of snuggeries (hiding places)

disparition (French) — disappearance

Ecce signum (Latin) — Behold the sign

homuncle (English) — a little man

Il n'y a pas d'épreuve. (French) — There is no proof.

irremeable (English) — offering no possibility of return

jarvey (English) — driver of a hackney coach

La jalouse se lève de bonne heure. (French) — The jealous woman rises early.

lustrum (English) — a period of five years

mensiversary (English) — commemoration of a month

On dirait une masque champêtre. (French) — One could say a rustic masked ball.

pauvrette (French) — poor little one

peu beau spectacle (French) — hardly a lovely sight

rentrée (French) — return

Spretasque (Latin) — and the spurned women

πρόσωπα [prosopa] (Greek) — theatrical mask

σχετλιος [schetlios] (Greek) — cruel or abominable

Color separations by Photolitho AG, Gossau-Zurich, Switzerland.
The text is set in ITC Cheltenham Book and the headings in Cheltenham
by Commerce Graphics, San Diego, California.
Interior and cover design by Sandra Darling and Judythe Sieck.
Printed at The Green Tiger Press, La Jolla, California.
Bound by National Bindery, Pomona, California.
The color plates were tipped in by hand at The Green Tiger Press.
The original illustrations were done in India ink, modeled with
ink washes, and overlaid with watercolors.

Manufactured in the United States of America